This book is dedicated to
Darren, Derek, and Conner—
our good and able crew

First it appeared to be a ridge of water

①

Then quickly it solidified as an object emerged

②

head on
↑ water bulges ↑ up on side

Deanna noted water bulged up on the sides of the object.

③

It looked to be moving very slowly "skulling" it's long tail like a muskrat

But I was sure now it wasn't a long log moving funny as it floated

④   apparent 25'

Then it's "head" rose out of the water. It was black + gray + shiny wet like a seal

I turned the boat or I stood to ⑤

look out the back off the stern
and the thing was moving
away — I saw a distinct V-wake

⑥

Then before our eyes at less than 150' — maybe only 100' — it submerged tail, body,
Then head (like an enormous turtle would)

⑦

up + down with

leaving a dying V wake and a vacancy ring on the surface.

⑧

⑨

→ Wawg a muskrat skulls along with its tail. We watched for 20 or 30 more seconds. It raised its blunt end a bit higher in the water. I saw it was gray and black and shiny as round as a soccer ball. It reminded me of a harbor seals' wet head. Suddenly I saw it swim, creating a "v" shaped wake as water parted around its round "head". It was no log. It was an animal with a round head and a long tail.

MONSTER HUNT

Exploring Mysterious Creatures with Jim Arnosky

DISNEY · HYPERION BOOKS
NEW YORK

First Edition
10 9 8 7 6 5 4 3 2 1
F850-6835-5-11032
Printed in Singapore
ISBN 978-1-4231-3028-4
Reinforced binding
Visit www.disneyhyperionbooks.com

INTRODUCTION

One summer night on Lake Champlain, I rowed out to my boat, *Crayfish*. The water was as still as the air and black as the sky. It was eerily quiet. Only my oars made any sound. As I rowed, I imagined the lake's legendary sea serpent, "Champ," suddenly emerging from the depths, and I wondered if all the lake-monster stories I had heard might be true.

Once aboard *Crayfish*, I turned on the sonar and watched the small screen for anything unusual—something other than the familiar shapes of fish swimming beneath the boat. Out in the dark, alone on my boat, thinking about monsters, I wasn't afraid. My mind has always been open to new possibilities in the animal world.

The science of studying reports of unknown animals is called *cryptozoology*. Cryptozoologists make it their business to wonder about and try to discover the truth behind these mysteries. The idea of finding a species of animal thought to have been extinct, or discovering a brand-new animal unknown to science, appeals to my sense of adventure.

What could be more thrilling than seeing a prehistoric reptile swim out of the murky past and splash into the present right before your eyes? Or glimpsing a magnificent creature like Bigfoot tramping through the forest? In this book, I wonder about these and other possibilities. I'm going on a monster hunt. Come along. Wonder with me.

—Jim Arnosky

Giant Sharks

It was my sense of wonder that made me a fisherman. I'm always wondering what kinds of fish live in different waters. I wonder how colorful they are, what they like to eat, and how big they grow. I love hearing stories of fish so big and strong that they break sturdy fishing rods into pieces. The largest fish I have ever caught was a six-foot-long lemon shark. The largest fish I have ever seen was a whale shark. It was nearly thirty-five feet long. I watched it swimming toward a seal floating on the surface, but the seal was not in any danger. Whale sharks feed only on plankton and small fish.

The largest shark ever to swim in the ocean was a true monster named *charcharodon*. Charcharodons grew to be fifty feet in length and could bite a whale shark in two. And though charcharodons are thought to have gone extinct at least 13,000 years ago, fishermen's stories of monstrously large sharks are told in chilling detail to this day. Could there be charcharodons still roaming the seas?

The answer may be found someday, not by cryptozoology, but by beachcombing. All sharks occasionally break and lose teeth. The teeth of living sharks are white. Fossilized teeth of prehistoric or extinct sharks are black or brown or gray. Ancient charcharodon teeth occasionally wash up on beaches, along with smaller fossilized shark teeth. If a white charcharodon tooth ever tumbled in with the waves, it would be proof that these monster fish still exist.

A charcharodon compared to a twenty-foot-long great white shark

GIANT SQUIDS

Go out on the open ocean, and it becomes abundantly clear that the world is big enough for monstrously large animals. There are huge fish such as the manta ray, twenty-two feet wide and powerful enough to haul a ship out to sea. There are whales as large as jumbo jets surfacing offshore. And there are gigantic squids with tentacles long enough to reach out of the water and pull down small boats.

Giant squids were once believed to exist only in the minds of those who claimed to have been attacked by them. Mariners returned home from sea telling frightening tales of ships crushed and mangled by the tentacles of fifty-foot-long monsters with large, glowing eyes. They called these creatures *kraken*.

The kraken is one mysterious creature from the unknown that became a known animal. Carcasses of giant squids have washed ashore, and pieces of giant squids have been found in the bellies of sperm whales. The first sighting of a living giant squid was recorded in 2004 by Japanese researchers.

We know very little about the life of giant squids down deep in the ocean. What we do know is that they are swift and strong and can catch and eat prey as large as swordfish. Their size, strength, and secretive lives make giant squids seem to be everything the ancient mariners said they were—true monsters of the deep. And the sailors were even right about the glowing eyes. The giant squid's glowing eyes are an example of bioluminescence—light generated from within an animal's body.

The old sailors' tales of the kraken were based in truth. Gorillas and Komodo dragons were also considered to be only the stuff of tall tales—until the mid-nineteenth century, when they were discovered to exist. The *coelacanth*, a fish thought to be extinct for millions of years, was found to be still living off the coast of Africa.

What about all the stories of lake monsters, and of forest creatures like Bigfoot? Could they be real animals like the giant squid, gorilla, Komodo dragon, and coelacanth?

My home state of Vermont is a land of forested mountains bordered on the west by the 120-mile-long Lake Champlain. We have had reports of both Bigfoot and lake-monster sightings. I learned about the Bigfoot sightings through conversations with hunters, farmers, and woodsmen. In every case, I know the teller of the tale to be trustworthy, and I believe he truly saw the forest creature he described. And while boating on Lake Champlain, my wife, Deanna, and I have twice seen something large and mysterious and alive moving in the water.

All of this has opened our minds to the fact that many monster sightings could truly be glimpses of some unknown animal or animals.

The totem shows a Komodo dragon and the prehistoric fish called a coelacanth (pronounced SEAL-uh-kanth). In the illustration is a magnificent silverback gorilla.

BIGFOOT

Bigfoot, Sasquatch, Skunk Ape, and Grassman are all names for the same mysterious monster believed by some to be a large apelike animal living in the forests and swamps of North America. Eyewitnesses describe Bigfoot as something like a giant gorilla that walks upright on two legs—seven feet tall, 300 to 400 pounds, and covered with thick black or brown hair.

An animal as large as Bigfoot would be an imposing figure in the wild. Occasionally it would encounter other equally large animals. Would a moose or a bear suddenly coming upon Bigfoot be frightened and run away? Would Bigfoot run in fear? Would both animals become defensive and threaten to fight? Or would each sense little or no danger and simply go about their business? Where would a large animal like Bigfoot live? In a cave like a bear, or in the open like a moose? These are the kinds of questions we need to ask ourselves if we are to believe Bigfoot is real.

There are many different descriptions of Bigfoot's face. Its eyes are either yellow or red, big or small, depending on the eyewitness. Its nose is pointed, pugged, flat, or round. Bigfoot has been described as having long hair and also as having short hair. It has been described as thin, fat, young, and old.

What the eyewitnesses all agree on is that Bigfoot walks on two legs and can move very quickly. One person I know described how Bigfoot hopped across a road in just two huge strides. Another saw an agile Bigfoot cross a wide, rushing stream, stepping quickly from boulder to boulder, its long arms swaying gracefully as it moved.

Bigfoot gets its name from the huge bare footprints it leaves behind. Scores of Bigfoot prints have been found and followed. Many have been cast in plaster to preserve them. Some of the casts have been dismissed as hoaxes. Others, though, have convinced some scientists that they were made by real, humanlike but nonhuman feet. Really big feet!

The totem shows some versions of Bigfoot based on different eyewitness descriptions.

When you think of Bigfoot as a real wild animal, it's fun to imagine how it would live. For instance, it could be omnivorous, like a bear or a raccoon. That means it could eat everything from green plants, berries, fruits, nuts, and roots to small animals like insects, frogs, and mice. Turtle and bird eggs could be Bigfoot food. And Bigfoot could also catch and eat fish.

Bigfoot would have to move quietly and stealthily in order to keep from being seen. This is not impossible. A large black or brown animal easily blends into a forest scene. I once watched a bull moose suddenly vanish by simply lying down behind some brush.

By living off the land and avoiding human contact, a scattered population of Bigfoot animals could be living in the vast wilderness of our forests and swamps.

For centuries, stories of sea serpents have captured people's imaginations, creating visions of ferocious water-dwelling dragons rising out of the waves. While they may be based on actual encounters, tales of these creatures seem more fantasy than reality.

The creatures that people describe having seen in Loch Ness and Lake Champlain seem more natural, less fantastic. In those and many other deep lakes across the globe, people have spotted what appear to be large aquatic animals. As nonthreatening as manatees or whales, but not manatees or whales. Unidentified. Mysterious. Yet very real.

THE LOCH NESS MONSTER

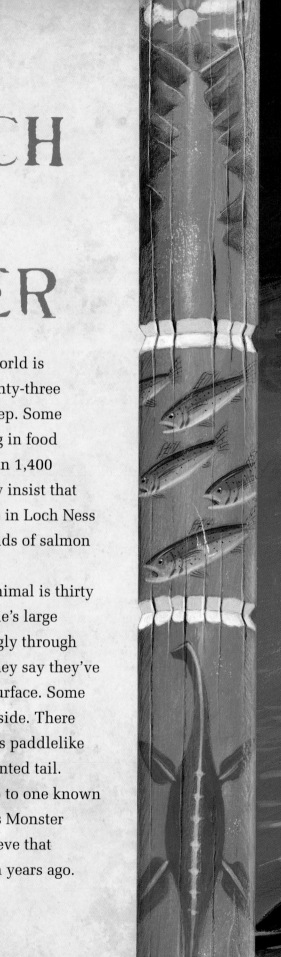

The most famous lake monster in the world is Scotland's "Nessie." Loch Ness is twenty-three miles long, one mile wide, and 800 feet deep. Some scientists say the lake is too cold or lacking in food to support a huge animal. But the more than 1,400 eyewitness reports suggest otherwise. They insist that some kind of mysterious creature does live in Loch Ness and could be feeding solely on the thousands of salmon that migrate through.

People who have seen Nessie say the animal is thirty to thirty-five feet long. They describe Nessie's large humped back surfacing and plowing strongly through the waves before gradually submerging. They say they've seen Nessie raise its long neck above the surface. Some have seen two Nessies, swimming side by side. There are descriptions of Nessie having enormous paddlelike flippers, a small, snakelike head, and a pointed tail.

All of the descriptions of Nessie add up to one known animal—a *plesiosaur*. Could the Loch Ness Monster really be a plesiosaur? Paleontologists believe that plesiosaurs became extinct seventy million years ago.

One hundred million years ago, plesiosaurs were numerous. These large aquatic reptiles moved through the water by flapping their huge flippers, the way sea turtles do. In fact, plesiosaurs looked a lot like sea turtles without shells. Some plesiosaurs were not much longer than sea turtles, growing to be only six feet long. Others reached enormous sizes, up to forty-six feet in length. There were short-necked plesiosaurs and long-necked plesiosaurs. All had sharp teeth for snagging and holding on to fish, their prey.

Being a reptile, a plesiosaur living in Loch Ness would have to be able to survive winter by hibernating in underwater caves or crevices that contain air pockets for the animals to breathe, the way frogs hibernate inside the crevices in rocky river bottoms. Or a plesiosaur could escape the cold of the winter Loch by migrating through the Loch's canal system to the sea.

As with Bigfoot, there have been Nessie hoaxes. Toy dinosaurs and even humps of hay have been placed in the Loch and photographed to look like Nessie.

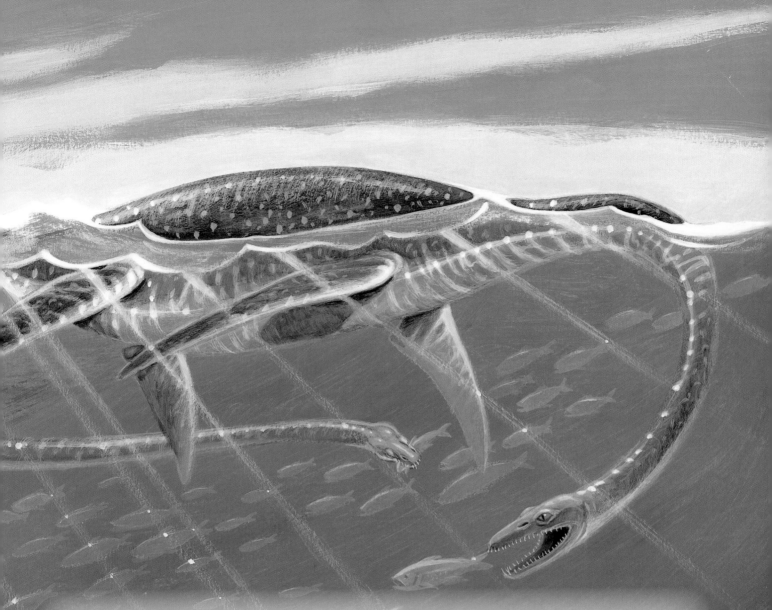

But for the most part, the reports of Nessie seem honest and sincere and have attracted the attention of serious researchers.

Scientific efforts to find Nessie have included sonar, remote-controlled submarines, and surface surveillance with binoculars and cameras. In a few cases some strange surface disturbances have been filmed and unexplained sonar soundings recorded. But the Loch is deep and dark, and in its murky water the mystery of Nessie remains well hidden.

THE LAKE CHAMPLAIN MONSTER

Lake Champlain lies between New York and Vermont and extends northward into Canada. It is named after the French explorer Samuel de Champlain, who sailed down the lake 400 years ago, logging all the plants and animals he saw. According to some historians, one of the animals he saw was a sea serpent. The Iroquois Indians, who knew the lake long before Champlain arrived, also spoke of a large serpent living in the water.

Over the years many more people have reported seeing what has been called the Champlain Sea Serpent or the Lake Champlain Monster. As with the sightings in its Scottish counterpart, Loch Ness, the majority of sightings in Lake Champlain describe an animal that fits the description of a plesiosaur. "Champ," as we now call the mystery animal, is said to be twenty to twenty-five feet in length, making it a slightly smaller version of Scotland's Nessie. And like Nessie, Champ has its believers and its skeptics.

Fossils of prehistoric animals in the rocks around Lake Champlain tell us that the lake was once part of a vast inland sea. The totem shows a trilobite fossil and three ancient species of fish that still live in the lake—gar, bowfin, and sturgeon.

Much bigger than Loch Ness, Lake Champlain is 120 miles long and thirteen miles across at its widest point. But it is only half as deep, at 400 feet. The deepest water is in the canyons and crevices in the vast and mountainous lake bottom. There are seventy-six islands and 580 miles of shoreline with scores of shallow bays. In these shallows an abundance of aquatic life can be found. But could a population of predators as large as the creature we call Champ survive just by feeding in the weedy shallows?

Aquatic weeds are edible by waterfowl, muskrats, deer, moose, and turtles. They also provide shade and hiding places for insects, crustaceans, fish, and amphibians. The lake's weedy habitats require a lot of sunlight to grow. Curious to see if any weeds or other aquatic food might be growing down deep where there is little or no sunlight, we set out in our boat *Crayfish* to explore.

To see the bottom of the lake you need to either dive down with a flashlight or lower a light-equipped camera. Deanna and I, along with our three hale and hardy grandsons as crew, lowered such a camera to the bottom of the lake, and what we saw amazed us! In water as deep as thirty feet, large mussels covered every square inch of the bottom—large freshwater mussels that are food for sturgeon, sheepshead, bass, and catfish. Plesiosaurs ate fish. Could they also have fed on mollusks like mussels, the way seals and otters do? Could an animal like Champ be eating mussels as well as fish?

I painted this scene bright so you could see the type of bottom we drifted over. Actually the water at thirty feet of depth is very dark.

26

In the small portion of Lake Champlain that we explored, we discovered a landscape of hills, valleys, flat plains, rocky cliffs, ledges, reefs, and submerged mountains. The underwater mountains, called *sea mounts*, were carved and created by slow-moving glaciers over 10,000 years ago. The mountains that rise above the water's surface form the lake's beautiful tree-covered islands.

We found deep, wide basins that held large schools of fish. We saw places where the ground under deep water gradually sloped upward to form shallow, weedy bays. And we saw that there were crevices in the rocky bottom that create mysteriously deep ravines. Most important, we learned that the lake provides everything an aquatic animal needs: food, freshwater, shelter under rock formations and inside natural crevices or sunken ships, and a refuge from surface wind and storms.

Lake Champlain is an underwater world big enough and rich enough to support a population of large predators, maybe even some as large as plesiosaurs. Could they go about their lives most of the time virtually unnoticed by land dwellers like us? They most certainly could.

At the end of the day, the crew of the *Crayfish* went over all the things we had learned about the lake—the new weeds, the mussel beds, the sea mounts, and what the islands looked like underwater. We remembered the deep holes we found that harbored large schools of fish. We talked about things each of us saw individually that the others might have missed.

Everyone was tired from hours of looking for Champ, both down deep with our underwater camera, and on the surface of the lake with our binoculars. We investigated everything that could have been mistaken for a large creature, such as floating logs or sticks. We saw how the motion of boats far away could send energy through the water all the way to where we were, creating long, dark, spooky waves resembling a monster.

Later that night, as often as I was asked, I told stories about the wildlife I have seen on the lake, and about the day Deanna and I saw something longer than our boat suddenly emerge just a hundred feet from our bow, and swim slowly on the surface before diving back down under.

The earth is home to many animals, and they go about their lives regardless of whether or not we know they exist. Right now, a Bigfoot family could be sleeping somewhere in the forest. Champ or Nessie could be swimming in the dark beneath a fisherman's boat.

New species of animals are discovered every year in the ocean, in distant rivers, and in remote forests all around the world. Keep an open mind. Today's mystery could be tomorrow's science. You may grow up to be the first marine biologist to study the habits and migration patterns of a rediscovered plesiosaur, or become a conservationist whose job is to protect the habitat of a newly discovered North American ape.

I hope we solve the mysteries of Bigfoot, Champ, and Nessie. And when we do, I hope new mysteries crop up to take their place. We need mystery.

June 29 2001 "Champ... a new anim...

— It is no lon...
regarding this thing people say they'v...
seen in Lake Champlain. Its a...
"What is it?" "What kind of animal is it...

— Yesterday, Deanna and I saw
something truly unbelievable in
Lake Champlain.

We were cruising south on the broad
Lake toward Bixby Island - to see where
the cormorants nest (and have despoiled all
the vegetation). The water was beautiful
calm. Deanna remarked "This is
Champ water"... because most of the
sightings of the mysterious creature of
Lake Champlain are made when the
water is still and calm.

— I was watching for floating debris....
logs, branches, and the like. I had
nearly hit a long waterlogged tree
trunk drifting just ~~~~ inches under
the waves earlier this spring.

— Suddenly, to my right at about
150 feet off the bow I saw what appeared
to be a long log drifting ~~~~ surface moving
~~~~ the gentle swells. As I watched, it
emerged higher in the water and I saw
it was ~~~~ tapered at
one end. "Look at that thing." I said
to Deanna. and very black in color ⊙

— together we watched as it rose a bit
more out of the water revealing a blunt/round
end ~~~~ long tapered end.

— It was strange in that it appeared
to be moving, sort of skewing on the
water with its ~~~~ tapered end, the

Anyone who has been on this broad lake in a choppy sea can tell
you you can't even see a small boat in it very easily. I wonder
if this animal could be out to expose more in a rough
sea... indicating a want that they are hidden by the same
~~~~ for what it would for prolation, it is... a use unlike one over what
we both can only decide as a gigantic 25' other here
~~~~ possibly just 15'. If one knew in a calm sea yesterday
at latitude 44°.47.649' and longitude 73°.19.427' a

This is where it happened
N 44°. 47. 649'
W 73°. 19. 427'
Brg. 228° Mag.
Distance 3.75 miles
from our cove.

2 miles east of La Roche Reef in 56 feet of water